GREETINGS, SHARKLING!

For three of my favorite Earthlings:
Tyler, Brett, and Aubrey
—L.H.H

To Bret and Suzie Warrick, who have always been there to rescue me from shark tanks
—J.W.

Galaxy Scout Activities illustrations by Nadia DiMattia

Library of Congress Cataloging-in-Publication Data

Houran, Lori Haskins.
Greetings, sharkling! / by Lori Haskins Houran ; illustrated by Jessica Warrick.
pages cm. — (How to be an earthling ; 2)
Summary: "Spork the alien learns about honesty after Jack tells him a lie on a field trip and Spork ends up swimming with sharks"— Provided by publisher.
ISBN 978-1-57565-822-3 (pbk) — ISBN 978-1-57565-821-6 (reinforced library binding) — ISBN 978-1-57565-823-0 (ebook)
[1. Extraterrestrial beings—Fiction. 2. Honesty—Fiction. 3. School field trips—Fiction. 4. Humorous stories.] I. Warrick, Jessica, illustrator. II. Title.
PZ7.H27645Gr 2016
[Fic] — dc23
2015009953

3 5 7 9 10 8 6 4 2

First published in the United States of America in 2016 by Kane Press, Inc.
Printed in China

Book Design: Edward Miller

CONTENTS

Don't miss a single one of Spork's adventures!

Spork Out of Orbit

Greetings, Sharkling!

Take Me to Your Weeder

Earth's Got Talent!

No Place Like Space

Alien in the Outfield

May the Votes Be with You

Money Doesn't Grow on Mars

GREETINGS, SHARKLING!

by Lori Haskins Houran
illustrated by Jessica Warrick

KANE PRESS
New York

Spork

Trixie Lopez

Mrs. Buckle

Grace Hanford

Jo Jo

Newton Miller

REPORT TO TROOP

BEEP. BEEP. BEEP.

Hey, guys! It's me, Spork!

You'll never believe this. I've been here for only three Earth days, and already I'm going on a special mission.

A FIELD TRIP with Mrs. Buckle's class!

I can't wait to visit an Earth field. I'll bet it's thrilling! I will send a full report later. This is SURE to help me get my Solo Explorer badge.

I'd better go now. Mrs. Buckle says we have to finish our homework to go on the trip. Lots to do . . .

Over and out!

1

A NEW KIND OF HOMEWORK

Newton hurried along the sidewalk. He walked so fast his glasses jiggled on his nose. Newton hardly noticed. He was too busy making sure he'd remembered everything for the field trip.

Did I pack my lunchbox? he thought. *Yes.*

Did I bring a sweatshirt just in case? Yes.

Did I finish my math worksheet? Yes.

But wait—did I put it back in my homework folder?

Newton stopped short. He flung his backpack on the ground and tugged at the zipper. The backpack opened with a wide yawn.

There was the worksheet, right where it was supposed to be. *Phew!*

“Greetings, Newton!” said a squeaky voice.

Newton looked up. Spork was waving hello from the top of his spaceship.

“Oh. Hi, Spork,” said Newton.

Spork seemed nice. Very nice, actually. It was just . . . Newton couldn’t quite get used to hanging out with a space alien.

Spork had landed on Earth a few days before—in the middle of the school playground! Mrs. Buckle had invited him to join the third grade, and right away the other kids seemed comfortable with Spork. Trixie played hopscotch with him. Grace shared her pencil box with him. And Jack—well, Jack picked on him, the way he picked on everybody.

Newton was pretty sure he was the only one who felt shaky around the little alien.

"Just finishing my homework!" Spork called down to Newton. "I didn't know how to do it at first, since my home is so far away. Then I thought, my spaceship is my home for now! So I worked on it all night. I dusted the plasma panels, scrubbed the proton boosters . . ."

Spork picked up a shimmery cloth. He rubbed the round window of his ship. "Looks good, huh?"

"Yes, but—" Newton began. Before he could say anything else, someone behind him started to laugh.

Newton turned around. Jack stood there, grinning.

"Is *that* what you thought *homework* was?" Jack said. "Ha! That's *hilarious*!"

Newton tried to ignore Jack. "Spork, homework doesn't mean working on your home," he said. "It's schoolwork you do there. Like the math worksheet Mrs. Buckle gave us yesterday."

Spork stopped wiping the window. "You mean, I *didn't* do my—"

RRRRRING! The bell rang for school.

"See you inside," Jack said. "I don't want to be late handing in my *homework*!"

Newton looked at Spork. The alien's orange face had turned a pale shade of peach.

"This is bad," said Spork. "Very bad. If

I didn't do my homework, I can't go on the field trip! What should I do?"

"I don't know," Newton said. "I guess you have to tell Mrs. Buckle what happened."

Spork made a small, unhappy squeak. Newton felt sorry for him. He had never had to tell a teacher he didn't do his homework. Just the thought of it made his heart flip-flop.

Spork followed Newton inside. Mrs. Buckle stood at her desk collecting papers.

Trixie and Grace handed in their worksheets.

"Good morning! Thank you, girls," Mrs. Buckle said.

Next it was Newton's turn. He took out his paper and gave it to Mrs. Buckle.

"Thank you, Newton," she said. "Spork, where's yours?"

"Well," began Spork. "What happened was . . ." He stopped.

Newton thought he heard Jack giggle.

"What happened was . . ." Spork said again. He looked right at Mrs. Buckle. "My flarg ate my homework."

Newton gasped. He couldn't believe it. Spork told a lie.

To a *teacher*!

2

I CANNOT TELL A LIE

"Spork," said Mrs. Buckle, "is that really what happened?"

Newton saw Spork's shoulders slump.

"No, Mrs. Buckle," Spork whispered. *"Please don't be mad!"* Newton didn't know he was going to say anything until the words flew out of his mouth. "Spork didn't do his homework because he had no idea what homework was!"

Newton told Mrs. Buckle about Spork's mix-up.

"It's okay, Spork," said Mrs. Buckle. "I'll let you do the homework here, so you can come with us on the field trip. But first, let's all take a seat on the carpet."

Mrs. Buckle waited until everyone was sitting quietly.

"I want to tell you a little story about George Washington. Can someone explain to Spork who that was?"

Grace raised her hand. "He was the first president of our country."

"Oh, like Varp Zerpingnut, the first leader of my planet!" said Spork.

"When George Washington was a boy," Mrs. Buckle began, "someone gave him a shiny silver axe. He loved that axe. He went around his yard chopping everything in sight—even his father's favorite cherry tree. George's father came home, and he was very angry. He demanded to know who had cut down the tree. George was

afraid, but he answered, 'I cannot tell a lie. I did it.'"

"What happened?" asked Spork. "Did he get in trouble?"

Newton was wondering the same thing.

"No," Mrs. Buckle said. "George's father told him, 'Your honesty is worth more to me than a thousand trees.' That's how I feel, too. Nothing is more important than telling the truth. Especially when it's hard or scary. Do you understand?"

Spork nodded. Newton and the other kids nodded, too. Everyone looked very serious.

"Good," said Mrs. Buckle. She smiled. "Now, who's ready for a field trip?"

Mrs. Buckle found an extra copy of the math sheet for Spork. He started working on it right away.

"The rest of you grab your lunchboxes and line up," said Mrs. Buckle. "I'll go get the treat I brought you. Homemade cookies!"

Mrs. Buckle's heels clicked out the door and down the hall.

"Oh, no," groaned Trixie.

"Not cookies!" moaned Grace.

Spork looked up from his paper. "What do you mean?" he asked. "I thought young Earthlings loved cookies."

"We do," explained Newton. "Just not Mrs. Buckle's cookies. They're not very good."

"They taste like sawdust, and they're hard as rocks," said Jack.

For once, Newton had to agree with him.

"Last time I bit one, I lost a tooth," Trixie added. "And it wasn't even loose!"

The kids lined up near the front door.

Newton found a spot in the middle of the line, between Trixie and Grace.

Just as Mrs. Buckle returned with the box of cookies, Spork finished the last problem on the math sheet.

"Done!" he said. He ran to the back of the line, right behind Jack.

"Great," said Mrs. Buckle. "Let's go!"

The third graders climbed on the bus. Newton and Trixie shared a seat.

Newton frowned when he saw Spork and Jack sitting together across the aisle. He hoped Jack wouldn't make fun of Spork again.

A minute later, he heard Jack laugh.

"Hey, guess where Spork thought we were going?" Jack called. "A field! Because it's a *field* trip! Ha!"

"Cut it out, Jack," said Trixie. "Spork, we're going to an aquarium. It's a place with lots of fish and water animals."

"Oh," said Spork. Newton could tell he was disappointed.

"But we'll pass some fields along the way," Newton said.

"Cosmic!" said Spork, brightening again.

The bus started up with a loud rumble.

"We're taking off!" squeaked Spork excitedly. "Prepare for launch!" He scrunched into a tight little ball. "Three . . . two . . . one . . . *BLAST OFF!*"

3

KER-PLOP!

The bus wheezed. It inched away from the curb and bumped along the street.

"Um, Spork?" said Newton. "Did you think we were going to *fly* to the aquarium?"

"Of course," Spork said, uncurling himself. "But this is much better! A *rolling* rocket. And it moves slowly so you can see the sights! I must suggest these for my planet."

Jack snorted, but Spork didn't seem to care. He was pointing out the window.

"Look at all the Earth dwellings! They're different colors. All the houses on my planet are silver!"

Spork stared out the window the whole way to the aquarium.

"Here we are!" said Mrs. Buckle. Everyone streamed off the bus and through the aquarium doors.

"Whoa!" said Newton, pushing up his glasses.

"Double whoa!" agreed Trixie.

They were standing in an enormous room. The sides of the room were lined

with tall glass tanks. They looked like windows into the sea.

On the left, a school of yellow fish darted in and out of a coral reef. On the right, a pair of manta rays glided past.

Newton bounced on his toes. He couldn't wait to see what was in the rest of the tanks!

“Feel free to explore this room, but stay with your bus buddy,” Mrs. Buckle instructed. “We’ll meet in front of the sea-turtle tank at eleven o’clock. Have fun!”

“Come on! Let’s go this way,” said Trixie, tugging on Newton’s sleeve.

“Okay!” said Newton.

Past the manta rays, they spotted tanks of seahorses and jellyfish.

“Aw, the seahorses are so cute!” said Trixie. “They really look like teensy horses.”

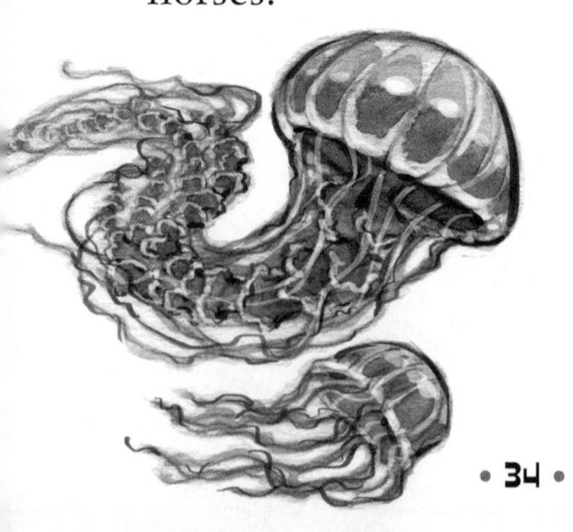

“Check out the jellies,” said Newton. He couldn’t believe how beautiful and strange they were. Some were bright blue with long strings trailing behind them. Some were see-through and glowed like eerie underwater nightlights.

The next tank held two large, squishy creatures with googly eyes. They each had eight arms and two long tentacles.

"Are those octopuses?" asked Trixie.

"Hey! SQUIDS!" cried Spork.

He ran up behind Newton and Trixie. Jack shrugged and kept walking.

"You know about squids on your planet?" asked Newton.

Spork laughed. It was a funny, tinkly sound, like the highest notes on a piano.

"Squids are *from* my planet," he said. "Hi, guys!"

The squids just kept swimming.

"Oh, they can't hear me," said Spork. He tapped on the glass and waved.

The squids waved back!

They looked happy to see Spork. They bobbed up and down in their tank and blew big bubbles.

"Oops, I have to catch up with my bus buddy," said Spork. He waved goodbye to the squids. "See you later!"

"Newton, are you okay?" asked Trixie.

Newton couldn't stop staring at the squids.

"Uh, sure," said Newton. He followed Trixie slowly to the next tank. But his head was spinning. Squids were from outer space?

It made sense, in a way. They looked like they could be from another planet. But a lot of animals looked strange. Were they aliens, too?

What about those glow-in-the-dark jellyfish? wondered Newton. *Or giraffes? Or aardvarks? Even their name is weird. . . .*

Newton was so deep in thought that he barely noticed Spork and Jack right next to him.

"When do we go swimming?" Spork asked Jack.

"Swimming?" said Jack.

"That's why we're here, isn't it? To swim with the water creatures?"

"Oh, yeah! Of *course,*" Jack said. "We're going to jump right in this shark tank. You can go first."

"Wait. *What?*" said Newton, snapping to attention. "Jack, don't lie to Spork!"

Jack laughed. "It's not like he's really going to—"

Ker-plop!

"What was that?" said Trixie.

Newton looked up.

"Oh, no!" he cried. *"SPORK IS IN THE SHARK TANK!"*

4

A SHARK SNACK

"W-what? But how—" stammered Jack.

"Go get Mrs. Buckle!" said Newton. "Hurry!"

Jack took off. Newton and Trixie ran up to the tank.

"Spork!" Trixie shouted. "Get out of there!"

"Please, Spork!" begged Newton.

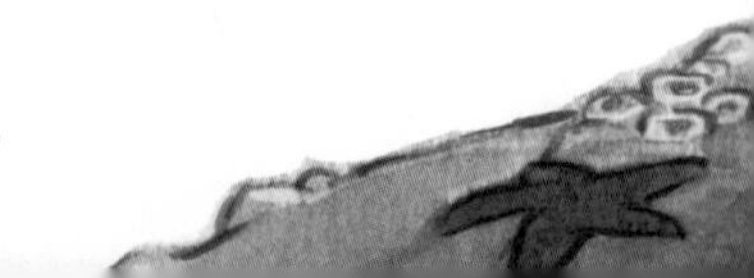

Spork couldn't hear them. He gave a cheerful thumbs-up. Then he pointed to the shark on the other side of the tank.

The very LARGE shark. With the very SHARP teeth.

"No!" cried Newton.

Newton and Trixie watched Spork swim up to the shark.

They watched Spork wave hello.

They watched the shark open its huge jaws and *LUNGE*!

"*Eeeeeeeeeeek!*" they shrieked, covering their eyes.

"What's happening?" said Trixie. "I can't look!"

Newton peeked through his fingers.

"Spork's dodging the shark!" he reported. "Left! Right! Up! Down! Oh, no—the shark has him trapped in a corner!"

"We have to help!" wailed Trixie. "We're Spork's *friends*!"

Newton tried to think fast. What could they do?

Then he remembered something—Spork's *other* friends, the space squids! Could they help?

He ran back to the squid tank. He banged on the glass.

"Look!" he shouted, waving his arms frantically at the shark tank. "LOOK!"

The squids turned their huge, googly eyes toward Spork and the shark.

Then they started sucking in water. Great slurps of it. Just when it seemed they might burst—

BLAM! They blasted the water out!

WHOOSH! They rocketed over the wall!

SPLASH! They landed in the shark tank!

One squid shot a cloud of thick black ink right in the shark's face.

"Yes! Go, squids, go!" yelled Trixie.

The other squid threw its tentacles around Spork. It started sucking in water again.

Then it blew Spork high out of the water. He sailed through the air—and over the side of the tank!

Newton and Trixie held out their arms.

"Gotcha!" cried Newton.

5

SAWDUST COOKIES

"What happened? What's going on?" Mrs. Buckle came rushing over with Jack.

"Sharks are MEAN," spluttered Spork. Newton and Trixie set him on his feet.

"No, *Jack* is mean," said Newton.

"He lied to you, Spork. We don't go swimming at the aquarium."

"Swimming?" cried Mrs. Buckle.

Jack looked down at the ground.

"Jack, we talked about honesty just this morning," Mrs. Buckle said. "And now you've told a lie. A lie that could have gotten Spork seriously hurt."

"I know," said Jack. His face was pale. "I never thought he'd get in the tank. Really. I didn't think he *could*. How—how *did* you get in there, Spork?"

"I jumped in, just like you said," Spork answered.

"But the wall of the tank is so high," said Trixie. "It's almost up to the ceiling!"

"That's not high at all," said Spork. "Not with Earth's weak gravity. See?"

Before they could stop him, Spork jumped straight up. He smacked the ceiling with his little orange hand. Then he landed lightly back on the ground.

"Wow!" said Newton.

"I'm sorry I lied to you, Spork," Jack said. "I won't do it again. I promise."

"Really?" said Spork.

"*Really,*" said Jack.

"C-cosmic!" said Spork. He was starting to shake all over. Little puddles of water were forming at his feet.

"My goodness, we need to dry you off!" said Mrs. Buckle.

"Here," said Newton. He was glad he

had brought a sweatshirt just in case! He untied it from his waist and wrapped it around the shivering alien.

"Th-thanks, Newton!" said Spork.

"You're welcome." Then Newton realized something. He wasn't nervous around Spork anymore! Not at all!

"I think we could all use a break,"

said Mrs. Buckle. "Let's go find the rest of the class."

Newton spotted Grace and the others by the sea-turtle tank. "There they are!" he said.

Mrs. Buckle counted the bus buddies by twos to make sure everyone was there. Then she led the class outside to the picnic area.

"Who wants a snack?" she said, opening her tote bag. "Spork, you can try one of my homemade cookies!"

"No, thank you, Mrs. Buckle," said Spork. "Newton told me they're not very good."

Newton's heart did a triple backflip in his chest.

"He did?" said Mrs. Buckle. She

looked at Newton in surprise. "Don't you like my cookies?"

Newton froze.

If he said no, he would hurt Mrs. Buckle's feelings.

But if he said yes, he would be lying to her!

What should he do?

Newton remembered George Washington and the cherry tree.

"I cannot tell a lie!" he burst out. "I don't like your cookies. They taste like sawdust, and they're hard as rocks!"

"Newton!" gasped Grace.

Newton clapped his hand over his mouth.

There was a pause.

A long, awful pause.

Mrs. Buckle pulled the box of cookies out of her bag. She took a cookie and bit into it.

CRRRRUNCH.

"Yuck!" she yelped. "And *ouch*! How did you kids eat these things?"

"It wasn't easy," said Jack.

"I had no idea," Mrs. Buckle said. Her cheeks were bright pink. "I never tried them. I was afraid if I ate one, I'd eat them all. I guess not! Newton, thank you for your honesty. I know it must have been hard to tell me."

"I should have found a nicer way to say it," Newton said miserably.

"Oh, honey!" Mrs. Buckle gave him a big hug. "You're right that it's best to tell the truth in a nice way. But saying these cookies taste like sawdust *was* putting it kindly! I'm proud of you. And now that I know the truth, I promise not to bake any more cookies for the class."

"Really?" said Newton.

"*Really,*" said Mrs. Buckle.

"Cosmic!" said Trixie.

Everyone laughed. Even Newton. He felt much better now.

Mrs. Buckle sighed. "What are we going to do with these terrible cookies?"

"I know!" said Spork. "We can feed them to my flarg. He'll be hungry. After all . . . he *didn't* eat my homework!"

REPORT TO TROOP

BEEP. BEEP. BEEP.

Great news! My special mission to the Earth field was a complete success!

No. Wait. That's not true.

I didn't visit a field after all. And I nearly got eaten by a very unfriendly Earth creature.

I haven't earned my Solo Explorer badge yet. But I will! I just know it!

Over and out.

P.S. Bob and Glaxklynak say hello!

ACTIVITIES

Greetings!

I am way, way smarter now than when I left on my mission! Now I know all this stuff about honesty. My Earthling teacher says, "Nothing is more important than telling the truth, especially when it's hard or scary." But that's not all there is to it—you need to be kind and think about feelings, too. It can get tricky so I made up a quiz about it. Give it a try!

—Spork

(There can be more than one right answer.)

1. Your flarg gobbles up your friend's lunch when she's not looking.
   a. You hope your friend won't notice.
   b. You grab your flarg and leave—fast.
   c. You say, "I'm sorry, but my flarg ate your lunch. Okay if we share mine and I bring you lunch tomorrow?"
   d. You say, "What happened to your lunch?"

2. Your friend is all excited. He says, "Look at my new kambax zoomer. Isn't it cool?" You look, and it isn't cool at all. You say:
   a. "Yeah, it's great."
   b. "I hate it."
   c. "I bet you have a lot of fun with it!"
   d. "Hey! Show me how it works!"

3. You broke the Galaxy Scout leader's plixit glass.
   a. You hide it.
   b. You tell him, "I had an accident with your plixit, and it broke."
   c. "Jarlish broke your plixit."
   d. "My flarg broke your plixit."

4. You find a brand new Snabble. You've always wanted one.
   a. Finders keepers. You stick it in your backpack and bring it home.
   b. You take it to Galaxy Lost and Found.
   c. You put up a sign: "Hey, somebody! Spork has your Snabble!"
   d. You hide it under a crellic bush. You'll come back for it when no one is around.

Answers:

1. The best answer is *c*. It's the truth, *and* you're making up for what your flarg did! In *a*, you're kidding yourself. Your friend will definitely notice—especially if lunch is gibbleburgers! In *b*, you're running away. *D* is a lie.
2. This is a tough one. *A* is a plain lie. You're telling the truth in *b*, and that's good, but I'll bet your friend's smile disappears when he hears it. Better to be nicer about how you feel. *C* is good because you're not lying or hurting your friend's feelings. But *d* is even better. You're making your friend feel good, and you might even have fun!
3. *B* is really scary but it's the only good answer. *A* is a lie—plus the Galaxy Scout leader will be looking all over for his plixit, when you know it's broken! *C* is a really mean lie because it could get somebody in big trouble. And in *d*, you're blaming your poor little flarg.
4. Hope you didn't choose *a* or *d*! How would you feel if you lost your new Snabble and someone took it? Both *b* and *c* are way better. *C* is my favorite because you'd be making the guy who lost it happy two times—once when he sees your sign and once when he gets his Snabble back!

SPOT THE TICKLING MISHIAN

If you're ever on planet Mishi, be careful! Half of its creatures keep to themselves, but half WILL TICKLE YOU IF THEY SEE YOU. The Mishians look a lot alike, but the Ticklers are different from the Non-Ticklers in small ways. Look at the pictures below and try to spot all the differences between the two Mishians. (There are eight.) I didn't notice and, yikes, they tickled me all the way back to my spaceship! And my little flarg, too.

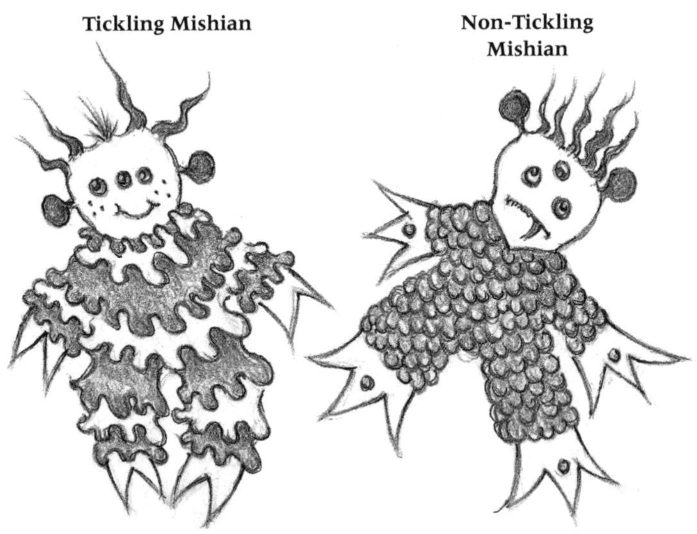

Answers: 1. The Tickling Mishian has a sprout of hair on top of his head. The Non-Tickling Mishian doesn't. 2. Tickler has three eyes in a row. Non-Tickler has three in a triangle. 3. Non-Tickler has a nasty fang. Tickler has none. 4. Tickler has freckles. Non-Tickler doesn't. 5. Tickler's ears are on the sides of his head. Non-Tickler's are on the top. 6. Tickler has two fingers and two toes. Non-Tickler has three fingers and three toes. 7. Non-Tickler has jewels on his hands and feet. Tickler's are bare. 8. Tickler has ruffles on his uniform. Non-Tickler has flat scales on his.

MEET THE AUTHOR AND ILLUSTRATOR

LORI HASKINS HOURAN has written more than twenty books for kids (not counting the ones her flarg ate). She lives in Florida with two silly aliens who claim to be her sons.

JESSICA WARRICK has illustrated lots of picture books about dogs, cats, and kids, but she is mostly interested in drawing aliens, for some strange reason. She does a pretty good job acting like an Earthling . . . most of the time.

Spork just landed on Earth, and look, he already has lots of fans!

★ **Moonbeam Children's Book Awards Gold Medal**
Best Book Series—Chapter Books

★ **Moonbeam Children's Book Awards Silver Medal**
Juvenile Fiction—Early Reader/Chapter Books
for book #1 *Spork Out of Orbit*

"Young readers are going to love this series! Spork is a funny and unexpected main character. Kids will love his antics and sweet disposition. Teachers and parents will appreciate the subtle messages embedded in the stories. The kids in the stories genuinely like each other, which I found refreshing. I will be giving these books to my young friends."—**Ron Roy**, author of A to Z Mysteries, Calendar Mysteries, and Capital Mysteries

"A breezy, humorous lesson in honesty that never stoops to didacticism. The other three volumes publishing simultaneously address similarly weighty lessons—lying, shyness, bullying, and responsibility—all with a multicultural cast of Everykids. . . . A good choice for those new to chapters."
—**Kirkus** for book #1 *Spork Out of Orbit*

"This is a book where readers, kids, and aliens learn together, experiencing how words and choices affect all of us. It's simple, elegant, and very insightful storytelling. *Greetings, Sharkling!* doesn't waste a single page of opportunity."
—**The San Francisco Book Review**

"I'm so glad Spork landed on Earth! His misadventures are playful and sweet, and I love the clever wordplay!"
—**Becca Zerkin**, former children's book reviewer for the *New York Times Book Review* and *School Library Journal*

"Kids will love reading about Spork. Parents, teachers, and librarians will love reading aloud this series to those same kids."—**Rob Reid**, author of *Silly Books to Read Aloud*

How to Be an Earthling

Winner of the Moonbeam Gold Medal for Best Chapter Book Series!

Respect

Honesty

Responsibility

Courage

Kindness

Perseverance

Citizenship

Self-Control

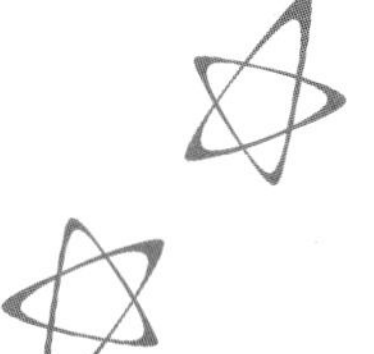

To learn more about Spork, go to kanepress.com

Check out these other series from Kane Press

Animal Antics A to Z®
(Grades PreK–2 • Ages 3–8)
Winner of two *Learning* Magazine Teachers' Choice Awards
"A great product for any class learning about letters!"
—Teachers' Choice Award reviewer comment

Let's Read Together®
(Grades PreK–3 • Ages 4–8)
"Storylines are silly and inventive, and recall Dr. Seuss's *Cat in the Hat* for the building of rhythm and rhyming words."*—School Library Journal*

Holidays & Heroes
(Grades 1–4 • Ages 6–10)
"Commemorates the influential figures behind important American celebrations. This volume emphasizes the importance of lofty ambitions and fortitude in the face of adversity…"*—Booklist* (for *Let's Celebrate Martin Luther King Jr. Day*)

Math Matters®
(Grades K–3 • Ages 5–8)
Winner of a *Learning* Magazine Teachers' Choice Award
"These cheerfully illustrated titles offer primary-grade children practice in math as well as reading."*—Booklist*

The Milo & Jazz Mysteries®
(Grades 2–5 • Ages 7–11)
"Gets it just right."*—Booklist,* starred review (for *The Case of the Stinky Socks*); *Book Links'* Best New Books for the Classroom

Mouse Math®
(Grades PreK & up • Ages 4 & up)
"The Mouse Math series is a great way to integrate math and literacy into your early childhood curriculum. My students thoroughly enjoyed these books."*—Teaching Children Mathematics*

Science Solves It!®
(Grades K–3 • Ages 5–8)
"The Science Solves It! series is a wonderful tool for the elementary teacher who wants to integrate reading and science."*—National Science Teachers Association*

Social Studies Connects®
(Grades K–3 • Ages 5–8)
"This series is very strongly recommended…."*—Children's Bookwatch*
"Well done!"*—School Library Journal*